Summer of Fire and Heart

a Firehawks Lookout romance story
by
M. L. Buchman

Buchman Bookworks

Other works by M.L. Buchman

Angelo's Hearth

Where Dreams are Born
Where Dreams Reside
Maria's Christmas Table
Where Dreams Unfold
Where Dreams Are Written

Deities Anonymous

Cookbook from Hell: Reheated
Saviors 101

Thrillers

Swap Out!
One Chef!
Two Chef!

SF/F Titles

Nara
Monk's Maze

1

Ashley Mason had gotten exactly what she asked for and was at a complete loss of what to do about it. The scenery from her fire lookout tower was incredible; the Bitterroot Wilderness stretched away in every direction. Rocky Mountains soared and steep-walled valleys plunged, all of it thick with pine trees of the darkest greens she'd ever seen.

Mount Sunflower—the highest point in her native Kansas at four thousand and thirty-nine feet, rising from the surrounding countryside by a whole nineteen feet—wasn't much higher than the valley floors here.

Her perch for the summer atop Medicine Point, which was the biggest mountain she'd ever been on, stood over two Kansases high with room to spare.

And she would kill for a latte right now. But the nearest refrigerator was a gazillion miles away, so no milk. She wasn't desperate enough to make one with non-dairy powdered creamer yet…but she was getting there.

The sky here was amazing, and she tugged down on her Kansas City Royals baseball cap so that she didn't have to see so much of it. The blue sky above went on almost as forever far as the green below and it was unnerving her.

It was all that cowboy's fault. There she'd been, happy as a pig in a poke to be out of Kansas. Paramus, New Jersey wasn't exactly the center of the universe, but it was such a relief from the endless flat of Hepler—a town that only existed because some fool had run two roads together out there in the middle of corn-fed nowhere with no thought about the trouble that would be causing future generations like hers.

She'd been aiming for the Big Apple, but

found an authentic Western wear boot shop in Paramus, New Jersey just before crossing the Hudson River and never quite finished the journey. It was just as well, her visits to the Big Apple almost convinced her that Hepler, Kansas wasn't so bad after all. But Ashley had dug in there just fine; not enough to plant roots, but just fine. She knew how to sell it with her Kansas accent, her track-and-field body, and her long blond hair. While there she'd accumulated a cheap apartment, an okay boyfriend, and a rattletrap Ford F150 that was now parked a three-hour hike down the mountain.

She'd been the queen of boot sales. No customer who came into the shop—especially not the really handsome ones—had managed to escape her clutches without a new pair of boots. It didn't matter how city they were; she could convince them that the only way to get a girl like her was with a fine pair of cowboy boots. Of course she never dated a customer, but she sure as shootin' knew how to sell them, each and every one.

Then that gorgeous cowboy had walked in, his Amarillo accent ringing so clearly of the great outdoors that he'd ruined Paramus for her in the first thirty seconds. Worse, he'd had a Brooklyn girlfriend with him and bought her a three thousand dollar pair of Lucchese hand-sewn boots. Ashley had always lusted after a pair of her own but even the employee discount didn't put them in range. And she knew that if the cards were flipped, she wouldn't want to end up with some hotshot city boy after all. She wanted…

Well. That was the problem. She'd didn't know, but she knew she wasn't going to find it in Paramus any more than she had in Hepler. She'd wanted out and had grabbed onto the first thing that was the opposite of selling cowboy boots to city folk who would wear them to a bar one time and then stuff them back behind their Pradas, Jimmy Choos, and Fratellis.

And she'd gotten her wish—some fairy godmother really had it in for her—nothing could be more opposite to Paramus than Medicine Point fire lookout. Five months. She'd signed up for five freaking months atop the Montana Wilderness.

The first day she'd been gobsmacked by

the wonder of it all. Days two through four had been setting up a routine and listening to her playlist—loud enough to drive out the silence…mostly.

Now it was day five and she was ready to bungee jump off her tower to end it all. The "cab"—her home for the next five months—was no bigger than a corn crib. The fourteen-by-fourteen foot box stood on stork-long legs of massive logs, twenty feet above the peak of Medicine Point. The summit was a craggy field with a couple of small campsites nearby, and then dramatic vertical plunges in every direction except the knife-edge trail that led back toward her truck.

Her nearest neighbor wasn't much closer than the nearest latte. Cougar Peak, The Lonesome Bachelor, and Old Crag lookouts were perched atop neighboring mountains, which meant they were twenty to sixty miles away. She could barely make out the towers through her big binoculars, never mind any people.

She stood on the narrow wrap-around catwalk, like a tiny summer veranda with a high porch rail. She leaned on it and looked down at the impossibly deep valley to the east. Any neighbor down there might as well be as far off as Paramus, except for her two days off every other week.

And it wouldn't do her any good even if she did come down off the mountain. The only towns within a hundred miles were no bigger than Hepler.

"Who knew that heaven would turn out to be such hell?" She asked the view. Gripping the catwalk rail until her knuckles went white, she screamed in frustration…and there was no one for miles around to hear her.

2

Brent Tucker nearly jumped out of his shoes at the scream that sounded just above his head. He'd thought he was all alone atop Medicine Point. Of course after the brutal hike up to the peak he hadn't exactly been focusing well.

He dumped his bundled-up hang glider—which had felt light enough five hours and three thousand feet ago—and looked upward. He'd walked right up beside the lookout tower to stare down off the rocky cliff edge at the jump he'd trudged so far to take.

Now he tipped his head back to look

up and saw someone standing on the cab's perimeter walkway with their head down buried against their arms on the rail. All he could really see of them was a royal blue baseball hat with the letters KC on the front in white.

"You okay?"

With a squeak of surprise the person raised their head and looked down at him. Even the shading of the hat couldn't hide the piercing blue eyes that inspected him in some alarm. Then her—definitely a her, a pretty enough her to tie his tongue in knots—long blond hair fell forward and hid her face.

"Who are *you?*" She didn't even try to wrestle the hair aside, so he guessed that she could see him even if he could no longer see her. He had traveled around the country enough to know that her accent wasn't Texas or Oklahoma. It was Kansas…but it wasn't. Somehow it sounded softer and smoother than any of them despite the flare of anger behind the question.

"Brent," as if that explained anything. "Tucker," which explained even less. "Brent

Tucker," he tried again, but talking to pretty women had always flummoxed him.

"Hi there, Brent." The "Hi" came out in a delicious cross of "Ha" and "Hey" and invited him to say something.

"Sorry to disturb you." *Sad, Brent. Real sad.* "I'll just set up and get out of your way. Shouldn't take more than thirty minutes."

"Thirty minutes?" She said it with a squeak of surprise and checked her watch. "Darn it!" And she disappeared from the rail.

He could hear her footfalls across the deck above him, but they stopped after a few moments, ending long before she could have reached the stairs down from her aerie. At a loss for what else to do, he began unbundling his hang glider. The faster he set up, the faster he'd be gone.

Once he had it out of the bag, he began piecing together the metal tubes for the wing edges and then the struts for the control bar. He had the wing fabric stretched and was just attaching the harness when a voice sounded close behind him.

"Sorry. I'm supposed to check for fire every half hour and I kinda forgot."

He spun to face her. Close up she had many amazing attributes. Tall enough to look him right in the eye, and a body in tight t-shirt and shorts proportioned to splendidly go with her height. Well-worn calf-high cowboy boots emphasized her long, muscular legs. Her blond hair was now back off her face, tucked through the rear hole in the ball cap. As pretty as she was, it was her eyes that commanded all attention. They were the same knockout blue as the Montana summer sky.

"What's that?" She moved to inspect his craft.

"A hang glider. Where have you lived that you don't know that?" *Continuing as smooth as ever, Brent.*

"Places where a molehill *is* a mountain. This—" she waved a hand at the vista, "I've never seen a thing like all this before jus' last week. Don't know as I ever want to again."

"Are you kidding me? This is glorious. I could look at this every day. This is one of the most unspoiled expanses of the forty-eight states. Every time I look at this I feel infinitely small and infinitely lucky. How can you not just love this?" *Now you're going out of your way to insult someone you don't even know. He should smack himself—would if he could figure out how to do it without looking even stupider.*

"I was already feelin' kinda small, and can't say as I'm much liking the help from the landscape." She turned from him to squint out at the horizon. "It's like it has secrets and no way does it plan on telling any of them, at least not to this girl."

"I'd think anyone would want to tell you their secrets."

Now she aimed that squint of inspection at him. He'd never flirted with a girl. He'd watched plenty of others do it, but his few attempts were always dismal failures. And now he was continuing his unblemished record of being an idiot around women.

His brain functioned on a perfect inverse proportional curve; the more attractive the woman, the more of a stumblebum he became. He'd managed to get up to the middle ground okay, where he could date a woman who was nice and fun to be with. But this Amazonian blond fire lookout was in an entirely different category and he was knocked right back into hopeless science geek.

To distract himself, he finished the inspection of his glider. Brent had planned to spend some time enjoying the view and he'd expected to spend a *lot* of time working up his nerve before jumping. He'd had plenty of lessons on smaller terrain, but this was to be his first major solo flight.

Under the fire lookout's watchful eye, he chose to simply strap in and get out before his congenital idiocy got the better of him. Someday he'd have to get over his awkwardness around attractive women, but this summer he had dedicated to mastering hang gliding. Maybe next summer he'd dedicate to learning how to speak to women…or studying to be a mime!

Without looking back, he clipped in, tipped up the wing, and ran for the cliff edge. Just as he launched into space, she called after him.

"My name is Ashley."

"Brent. Brent Tucker," he shouted back, which he'd already told her. By the time he'd thought to say more, he'd nosedived off the edge, rapidly gaining enough speed to properly fly and she was long out of earshot.

The nylon wing snapped brightly in the wind as it filled and took shape. The wind was loud without roaring.

He had flown well away from Medicine Point before he thought to look back. He could still see the tall woman with the wind-blown flag of sunshine hair despite the distance.

With a banked turn he lost sight of her.

It didn't matter. He wouldn't be seeing her again. He'd climb some other peak for his next flight.

Then it struck him with surprise, he was flying clean without all the nerves that had plagued his last two sleepless nights and the whole climb up the mountain. He banked again to follow the line of Warm Springs Creek ever so far below.

Though he wouldn't mind if he did see her again…maybe next time he'd pre-plan a few sentences so that he could at least pretend they were having an actual conversation.

3

Ashley couldn't help giggling a little to herself as "Brent, Brent Tucker" had flown away. It had been a long time since she'd struck a man speechless. It was a nice compliment, and a surprising touch of reality here in the vast wilderness. Maybe she could do this.

She watched the bright blue-and-black wing dip and soar against the background of pine green and rock as he swooped along. Even after he was out of sight she watched the wilderness, wondering what it would be like to feel so free.

Hepler and Paramus had been so crowded.

The former with all of her high school classmates who had just assumed that she'd settle down with one of them to be a farmer's wife. And the latter with so many Yankees that even the sound of her own thoughts had seemed those of a foreigner from a strange land—she'd kept adding more and more Texas to her accent just so that she still sounded like herself.

For an entire summer she would be utterly free. Able to think and do what she wanted. Well, except for every half hour. She glanced at her watch.

"Darn it!" Ashley raced back up the tower stairs, ten minutes late for her survey for forest fires.

4

It had been a week since Brent had flown away from Medicine Point vowing never to return. And his vow was still firmly in place, even as he hiked the last stretch up to the summit for his second time. But in the week since, he'd obtained his H3 intermediate license and traded up his floater wing to an intermediate rig. It had a narrower but longer wing and he couldn't wait to test the performance off a big hill instead of a small training slope. And his best flight yet had been off Medicine Point.

Of course, the intermediate wing weighed

another fifteen pounds more than the novice rig. Every step up the trail he'd cursed not choosing paragliding. The oversized parachute weighed under forty pounds, not over seventy, but he liked the feel of flying like a plane. Too late to switch, he'd already taken three weeks of lessons and summers didn't last forever no matter how much one wished them to.

As he approached the summit his steps slowed to even more of a crawl than they had while trudging up the long grade. The cab came into view and he could see her there behind the cab's big windows. She, Ashley, had her binoculars raised and was looking off into the distance.

The day was silent. A small flock of sparrows fluttered by in a quick twitter and a swallow soared about on the soft breeze in loops and swirls like a painter attempting to color the sky.

Ashley moved quickly and he could hear her voice clearly. She was practically shouting, "This is Medicine Point lookout. I have a smoke at six-three degrees. I think it's on the face of West Goat Hill."

A smoke?

A fire?

He scanned the horizon quickly but didn't see any flames approaching.

"This is Cougar Peak," another woman's voice crackled over the radio. "I confirm. One-two-zero for the cross, definitely West Goat. Strong white already going ash gray. Growing fast. Command, you'll want to get a team in there. Credit for sighting to Medicine Point. That's the first one of the season; I guess we all owe you a round when we get down in the fall. Your first fire makes you an official member of the club. Well done, Medicine Point."

"Thanks. That means I get to name it. Right?"

"You do. But we already had a West Goat Fire a couple years back."

Brent had eased his load to the ground and decided to brave the lookout tower to see the fire, and drag Ashley to safety if necessary. He was halfway up the steps when he heard Ashley's voice again.

"How about…" she trailed off.

Brent reached the cab's open door and

raised a hand to knock, when she turned and spotted him.

"Flyer Tuck!" she exclaimed in surprise.

"Where in the world did you get that, Medicine Point?" The woman on the radio continued without waiting for an answer, "Okay, it's officially the Flyer Tuck Fire. Cougar Peak out."

Brent knew his jaw was down, but there was nothing he could do about it.

Ashley looked from him, down to the radio in her hand, and back at him.

"W'all howdy, Flyer Tucker. It seems you've gone and gotten famous. My first one! You're on fire, boy. Better yet, you *are* a fire." Her laugh was high and wholehearted, impossible to resist.

Brent couldn't help himself and joined in.

Ashley set down the radio, crossed the cab in three steps, then she threw her arms around his neck and kissed him. She'd clearly meant it to be a quick, smacking kiss. The joy was just vibrating off her.

To keep himself steady—actually to keep her impact from driving him backward out the door and head over heels down the steep steps—he grabbed onto her waist. Somehow that quick smack of lips turned into an embrace and kiss that quickly dusted his prior experiences. Kissing Ashley was a more energized and exciting experience than full-on hot-and-sweaty sex with anyone in his past.

"Wanna see?" She pulled back from his arms as if nothing had just rocked his world and, taking his hand, dragged him to the huge windows that surrounded the small room.

It was an efficient space. There was a cot and a cooler beneath a cook stove. A line of counters down ran one wall and turned into a desk by the door, a tiny bookcase was crammed with novels. Squeezed in by the foot of the cot were two small armchairs. One of those big circular fire spotter tools took up the center of the cab—he paused long enough to spot a label, Osborne Fire Finder, before Ashley dragged him the rest of the way to the window. The cab was small enough that there was only a narrow walkway between the device and the furniture lined up along the walls.

"There!"

Brent followed the direction she was pointing, but he wasn't sure what he was looking for.

"Here!" She shoved a pair of binoculars into his hands with the same enthusiasm she had kissed him. Then she guided him until he saw it: a small column of smoke climbing up and dissipating quickly.

"Not much of a fire." He didn't know whether or not he should feel hurt that something so small had been named after him.

"That's," she turned toward the Osborne Fire Finder, whirling quickly enough that he was briefly lost in a cloud of blond hair, "eleven miles away. I bet it's a couple of acres already. Sit. Sit. I can't wait to see my first air show."

"Air show?"

"Shh," she kicked a pair of stools out from under the counter. She perched on one and, taking his hand once again, pulled him onto the other stool to sit beside her. Neither did she release his hand, instead keeping it trapped between both of hers.

He looked at the sun. It was still early in the afternoon. He could wait a while, he'd just have a shorter flight than he'd planned. Besides, he liked the way it felt…as if they were already friends. As if they'd known each other a long time.

"What's an air show?" He whispered his question because suddenly the cab felt a little like a holy shrine. She was so intent that she created an immense stillness in the space.

She just shook her head, unleashing a shower of hair about her face and shoulders.

5

"There," Ashley saw it and pointed, causing their shoulders to bump together as they sat side by side.

"All I see is a big bird that…" Brent's voice trailed off.

He had a nice voice once he used it. He was a funny mixture. She'd always gone for tall and big shoulders. He was neither, but it looked good on him. His dark brown hair was long enough to make a girl want to run her fingers through it and the close-trimmed beard gave him solid, reliable look that she rather liked. Brent matched her five-ten and was just a normal-looking guy—strong but no football star.

As they sat here, she'd finally figured out that he was embarrassed to be around her. On his first visit, she'd been so frantically glad to see another face that she'd been a little ridiculous, nothing new for her. He'd certainly flown the coop fast enough. It was one of the reasons she was keeping his hand pinned between hers at the moment—she didn't want him flying away again so quickly.

"…that's no bird." He reached for the binoculars, but she didn't let go of his hand so he had to fumble for them. With her free hand, she pulled out a second, smaller pair for herself.

She also didn't want to let go because she was *so* glad to see another human being. If her first five days had made her crazy, an additional week atop Medicine Point had nearly tipped her into the deep end. Except the last day or so she'd started enjoying it more, going for a trail run before watch duty, and the dinnertime sunsets were spectacular.

But the real reason she was holding on was that she was having trouble breathing and was half afraid she'd hyperventilate and faint if she did let go.

It was crazy.

All she knew about him was his name, that he had a hang glider, and that he kissed like they did in the movies. Star-spangled fireworks only happened on the big screen, but having an airshow for follow-up was pretty darned impressive in her cowgirl's experience and his kiss had earned every diving run of it.

First a small plane flew in and circled high above the fire, little more than a black dot in the blue sky. Ten minutes later a big plane roared by close overhead Medicine Point, making both her and Brent duck and laugh a little nervously. It dove down into the valley and then climbed across the face of West Goat Mountain. It dumped a long shower of water and turned back to race away over their heads again, returning to base for another load.

They had to wait twenty minutes before the next event, then the air was suddenly cluttered with aircraft.

First, the huge tanker aircraft returned

to dump another load, bright red retardant this time. Next, a smaller plane, painted black with red-and-gold flames down the side, flew overhead. In moments a half-dozen parachutes were floating down toward the fire. A pair of helicopters in the same paint scheme began flitting in and out over the fire dumping water or retardant as well.

"Look, you can see the flame now." It was both exciting and horrifying. She could easily cover the fire and most of the smoke with her thumb held out at arm's length. But there were trees burning and, more importantly, people down in that mess.

She barely remembered to check the rest of the horizon every thirty minutes—a pattern that was finally becoming a habit. The rest of the time she just sat close beside Brent.

They started talking about the fire and the air show; neither of them had ever seen anything like it. He was from Colorado, the eastern part, which wasn't all that much different from eastern Kansas. He'd graduated from the University of Montana.

"I'm not there yet," she told him. "I did night school online and have two years of credits." She'd never told that to anyone; it had always been her own private goal. "That was my ticket out of Paramus and a bonafide guarantee that I'd never go back to Hepler. With me gone, Hepler is down to a hundred and thirty-*one* people. The nearest high school was fifteen miles away. That's why I did so well at track-and-field. In addition to practice I rode my bicycle both ways to school because there was no late bus."

"We should go visit Lamar someday. It's huge!" Brent spread his arms wide, accidentally bumping her on the head. "At least by comparison. Seven thousand people. Impressed?"

"Terribly!" She clasped her hands to her chest as if about to swoon with delight. They no longer held hands, but still sat close enough that she could feel him there beside her. "What is a Colorado flatlander doing with a hang glider?"

The air show was fading along with the light. The fire was reported as contained and now just needed beating all the way down.

"I," Brent looked out the window, but she

couldn't quite tell what he was looking at.
"It'll sound stupid."

"I'm a Kansas farm girl who sold cowboy boots in Paramus, New Jersey. Top that one. I dare you."

6

Brent kept looking, but it wasn't dark enough yet. He couldn't see the reflection on the inside of the cab's glass—the reflection of a man he wouldn't recognize sitting next to…

He cleared his throat, still convinced that this wasn't really happening.

"I'm a first year professor at UM. They kept me on after my grad work; I teach undergraduate astronomy."

"Which has what to do with hang gliding?" Ashley's tone was light. She made it easy for him to talk and with the fading light he was slowly becoming less daunted by her beauty

and more enamored of her innate warmth of
heart.

"I…" *In for a penny, Tucker, in for a pound.*
"My dad said I'd never amount to crap," he
said it fast so that he wouldn't sound bitter.
"Probably because he hadn't either. I decided
that every summer—while school was out—I
would learn something new, really learn
it, to prove him wrong. I started a couple
years back. I spent a summer learning to
do long-distance bike riding, made it to
Wisconsin and back. I worked a summer with
a swim coach until I won a couple of amateur
competitions. I did ballroom dancing last
year. This year I decided to try hang gliding.
I've got my H3—there's only one more level of
licensing, but the H4 is a lot of work." Crap!
This was making him sound like he had no
direction at all. He loved teaching astronomy
and working with the kids. It was—

"Ballroom dancing?" Ashley sounded
aghast.

Perfect. She was one of those people who
thought that meant he was some sort of pansy
who—

"However did you talk to women who

were your dance partners? I'm not sure how you're talking to me."

Not the response he'd been expecting.

Ashley kept proving that in addition to being beautiful woman, she was also a very insightful one.

"Um, I just focused on the dance. Started with a male teacher so that I could learn the woman's role and understand how I should be guiding her. Then all I talked about with any partner was the dance. And…I have no answer for your second question. You're just the type of woman who scares the crap out of me. Let's just call it temporary insanity."

She watched him closely for a long moment before speaking, long enough that he wondered if she'd ask him to leave.

"Show me."

"Show you what? Why I can't talk to you?" How was he supposed to do that when he was?

"No. Show me how to dance."

And, much to his surprise, he did. In slow, careful steps, they worked a basic waltz step around and around the narrow space between counter and the Osborne Fire

Finder. The sunset filled the cab's windows with gold, reds, and finally deep purples. When the only lights outside were a tiny spot of brightness from the distant fire and the rising moon, she lit a candle lantern. He could see their reflections inside the glass as they moved more and more in sync about the tiny space.

His awareness of her grew until it was more than an ache or a need. It grew until he was conscious of nothing else but the warmth and softness of her beneath his hands, of the wild, fresh smell of her, and of the musical ring of her soft voice as she took over counting the time and steps. They moved from the slow waltz to the Viennese. She flowed easily into the quick Irish and finally the almost slouching country-western waltz.

They staggered to a halt after the world outside had gone completely dark, and only the flickering candlelight coaxed the blue from her eyes.

How long they stood in the perfect frozen silence together, he didn't know. Then she stepped back out of his arms.

He had brought no sleeping bag or blanket,

he'd expected to be back off the mountain still in the heat of the day. Where would he—

Brent's thoughts stumbled to a halt as Ashley reached down to her waist and then pulled off her t-shirt. Her bra was the same color as her eyes, and all he could do was stare in bewilderment as that too hit the floor.

When she stepped back into his arms, she moved all the way in. Her skin was a silken wonder and for just a moment as their lips first met, he looked at their reflection in surprise.

Then any thoughts other than the woman in his arms simply flew away into the night.

7

June slid into July then August. Ashley could only look out at the wilderness in wonder as each day dawned.

How had she ever felt alone in the Montana Wilderness?

Brent's schedule had slowly slipped around until he flew in the mornings and then hiked back up in the afternoon to lie in her arms. Sometimes they'd sit out on the catwalk for hours, staring up at the stars as he told her the stories of heroes and gods in the constellations. Other nights he'd tell her about spectral colors, fusion byproducts, and Doppler effects.

After feeling lost for so long—ever since the third day of her freshman year when she'd suddenly realized the small-town dead-end nature of Girard High School and Hepler, Kansas—she now felt as if the future was rushing toward her. She could practically hear it in the slow steadiness of Brent's breathing as he slept wrapped around her on the narrow cot. It was there in the sweetest of wake-up kisses, and in the little treats he would carry up the mountain with him for their meals—even one-cup cartons milk for her lattes, bless his soul.

On her alternate weekends down the mountain, he taught her to fly. She wasn't ready to tackle Medicine Point, but she'd flown beside Brent for three hours on an amazing updraft finally landing in the University of Montana track field.

She could feel him coming up the trail as she scanned the far hills to the south. Heard the slight clank as he dropped his packed glider at the foot of the tower and the vibrations as his feet climbed the wooden steps up to her.

He slipped up behind her, wrapped his arms around her waist, and held her close as she finished the slow turn and fire scan. He'd learned not to interrupt her or she'd lose her place in scanning the hills. The fire season had heated up and it was a rare day that someone didn't find a smoke. Her own count stood at twelve—in the upper third of the lookout pack, which didn't do her ego any harm.

But even his slightest touch left her needing all of her willpower to finish the job. When she did, and had turned and received a proper greeting, he pulled open his pack.

"Fresh bread. Aged cheese. Chocolate. Bubbly," he held up a bottle of sparkling cider. "I thought about bringing champagne, but I couldn't figure out how to keep it cold enough."

"What's the—" Then she stopped. She knew. Brent was such a romantic. It was three months today since he'd jumped off the cliff to get away from her. Of course he would celebrate their first meeting, even if it was an embarrassment to him, rather than their first dance or the first time they slept together. As she often told him, he really was too sweet for her own good.

She thanked him a little more thoroughly this time.

Then he held up a letter, "I checked your mail, like you asked."

8

Ashley's eyes went wide and then she looked aside and blushed.

Over the last three months Brent had learned a great deal about Ashley. And one of the things he'd learned was that she was almost impossible to embarrass. Her heart was so generous that it had let him in and there wasn't a sneaky bone in her body, but there was also a frank straightforwardness that didn't flinch aside from anything.

Yet here she was blushing bright red over a letter from his school. He'd wondered at it for the whole hike up. His summer was almost over. Hers would be too, whenever they closed the fire lookouts for the season, perhaps in another month.

He didn't know what he wanted to happen, but he couldn't imagine a life without her in it. They hadn't talked of the future, not a single word, too overwhelmed by how incredible the present felt. The return address on that slim envelope had suddenly dropped the future right into the center of his thoughts.

"It's…" she took it slowly from his nerveless fingers. "It's just this crazy idea I had. I didn't mean it to—" Then she tried again, but still wouldn't meet his eyes. "I just kind of hoped—"

Brent stopped her from wholly turning away by placing a hand on either shoulder. He tried not to hope that she'd done what he'd been praying for the entire hike up the mountain. He pulled out the pair of stools they had sat together on to watch the first of many firefighting air shows. He had to guide her onto one as he sat on the other.

"Just open it. Then we'll talk about what it means."

She nodded without looking up, her hair

showering forward and hiding her face just as it had the first time he'd ever seen her. She fumbled at the envelope several times and then finally just shoved it into his hands.

Ashley didn't speak, didn't look up as he worked the seal.

Careful not to look at the contents, he tried to hand the open envelope back to her, but she refused.

He rested a hand on hers and it was shaking.

Unsure of what else to do, he pulled out the single sheet. He started reading it aloud.

"Congratulations," was as far as he got before she screamed just as loudly as that first time and then clapped both hands over her mouth.

Now she looked up at him and he brushed back her hair so that he could see the most amazing eyes there ever were.

"I hoped," she mumbled. And now her eyes pleaded with him, awash with unfallen tears. "I hoped so hard."

He read on against the tightening in his own throat. "School of Physical Therapy and Rehab. Track and field scholarship. Late start authorized at end of fire lookout season." He couldn't believe it. She'd be at UM with him. Ashley Mason wanted to be—

"I won't take it if you don't want me there," she spoke in a rush. "I didn't want to presume. But the way we—" she tried to hang her head again, but he stopped her with a finger on her chin. "I wanted," she finally choked out as the first tears fell. "I so wanted."

Brent couldn't help smiling. He too had hoped so much. And then in a fashion that he'd barely managed believe, he had taken action himself.

"I have just two questions, Ashley Mason."

She nodded furiously and covered her eyes in alarm and then uncovered them again without speaking.

"I know that it's too soon, but I couldn't stand the thought of you not being in my life." He pulled the last thing from his pack, a small velvet ring box. He opened it to reveal the small sapphire. "It was the closest I could find to the incredible color of your eyes. I want to look at them every day for the rest of my life. Please say yes."

She looked from his eyes, down to the

ring box, and back. She opened her mouth, but nothing came out. After her third attempt, she just nodded. He had to hold her hand steady so that he could slip the ring on it. It looked far better there than he'd imagined possible.

He had to duck to kiss her as she kept staring down at it.

When at last she looked up at him, he had to struggle to find his own voice.

"My second question, and this is the important one…"

A look of worry slipped into her eyes and she clamped down her grip on his hands.

"We both learned so much this summer," he rubbed a thumb over the ring on her finger. "How, my beloved Ashley, do you feel about learning river rafting next summer?"

Her laughter, as sparkling bright as the sky above the Montana Wilderness, told him that he'd learned how to do this exactly right.

About the Author

M. L. Buchman has over 40 novels in print. His military romantic suspense books have been named Barnes & Noble and NPR "Top 5 of the year" and Booklist "Top 10 of the Year." He has been nominated for the Reviewer's Choice Award for "Top 10 Romantic Suspense of 2014" by RT Book Reviews. In addition to romance, he also writes thrillers, fantasy, and science fiction.

In among his career as a corporate project manager he has: rebuilt and single-handed a fifty-foot sailboat, both flown and jumped out of airplanes, designed and built two houses, and bicycled solo around the world.

He is now making his living as a full-time writer on the Oregon Coast with his beloved wife. He is constantly amazed at what you can do with a degree in Geophysics. You may keep up with his writing *and get exclusively free short stories* by subscribing to his news-letter at: www.mlbuchman.com.

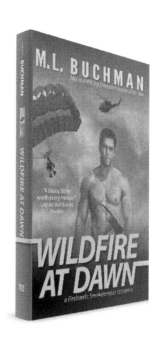

Wildfire at Dawn
(Book #1 of the Firehawks Smokejumpers trilogy excerpt)

Mount Hood Aviation's lead smokejumper
Johnny Akbar Jepps rolled out of his lower bunk
careful not to bang his head on the upper. Well,
he tried to roll out, but every muscle fought
him, making it more a crawl than a roll. He
checked the clock on his phone. Late morning.

He'd slept twenty of the last twenty-four hours and his body felt as if he'd spent the entire time in one position. The coarse plank flooring had been worn smooth by thousands of feet hitting exactly this same spot year in and year out for decades. He managed to stand upright...then he felt it, his shoulders and legs screamed.

Oh, right.

The New Tillamook Burn. Just about the nastiest damn blaze he'd fought in a decade of jumping wildfires. Two hundred thousand acres—over three hundred square miles—of rugged Pacific Coast Range forest, poof! The worst forest fire in a decade for the Pacific Northwest, but they'd killed it off without a single fatality or losing a single town. There'd been a few bigger ones, out in the flatter eastern part of Oregon state. But that much area—mostly on terrain too steep to climb even when it wasn't on fire—had been a horror.

Akbar opened the blackout curtain and winced against the summer brightness of blue sky and towering trees that lined the fire-fighter's camp. Tim was gone from the upper bunk, without kicking Akbar on his way out. He must have been as hazed out as Akbar felt.

He did a couple of side stretches and could feel every single minute of the eight straight days on the wildfire to contain the bastard, then the excruciating nine days more to convince it that it was dead enough to hand off to a Type II incident mop-up crew. Not since his beginning days on a hotshot crew had he spent seventeen days on a single fire.

And in all that time nothing more than catnaps in the acrid safety of the "black"—the burned-over section of a fire, black with char and stark with no hint of green foliage. The mop-up crews would be out there for weeks before it was dead past restarting, but at least it was truly done in. That fire wasn't merely contained; they'd killed it bad.

Yesterday morning, after demobilizing, his team of smokies had pitched into their bunks. No wonder he was so damned sore. His stretches worked out the worst of the kinks but he still must be looking like an old man stumbling about.

He looked down at the sheets. Damn it.

They'd been fresh before he went to the fire, now he'd have to wash them again. He'd been too exhausted to shower before sleeping and they were all smeared with the dirt and soot that he could still feel caking his skin. Two-Tall Tim, his number two man and as tall as two of Akbar, kinda, wasn't in his bunk. His towel was missing from the hook.

Shower. Shower would be good. He grabbed his own towel and headed down the dark, narrow hall to the far end of the bunk house. Every one of the dozen doors of his smoke teams were still closed, smokies still sacked out. A glance down another corridor and he could see that at least a couple of the Mount Hood Aviation helicopter crews were up, but most still had closed doors with no hint of light from open curtains sliding under them. All of MHA had gone above and beyond on this one.

"Hey, Tim." Sure enough, the tall Eurasian was in one of the shower stalls, propped up against the back wall letting the hot water stream over him.

"Akbar the Great lives," Two-Tall sounded half asleep.

"Mostly. Doghouse?" Akbar stripped down and hit the next stall. The old plywood dividers were flimsy with age and gray with too many showers. The Mount Hood Aviation firefighters' Hoodie One base camp had been a kids' summer camp for decades. Long since defunct, MHA had taken it over and converted the playfields into landing areas for their helicopters, and regraded the main road into a decent airstrip for the spotter and jump planes.

"Doghouse? Hell, yeah. I'm like ten thousand calories short." Two-Tall found some energy in his voice at the idea of a trip into town.

The Doghouse Inn was in the nearest town. Hood River lay about a half hour down the mountain and had exactly what they needed: smokejumper-sized portions and a very high ratio of awesomely fit young women come to windsurf the Columbia Gorge. The Gorge, which formed the Washington and Oregon border, provided a fantastically target-rich environment for a smokejumper too long in the woods.

"You're too tall to be short of anything,"

Akbar knew he was being a little slow to reply, but he'd only been awake for minutes.

"You're like a hundred thousand calories short of being even a halfway decent size," Tim was obviously recovering faster than he was.

"Just because my parents loved me instead of tying me to a rack every night ain't my problem, buddy."

He scrubbed and soaped and scrubbed some more until he felt mostly clean.

"I'm telling you, Two-Tall. Whoever invented the hot shower, that's the dude we should give the Nobel prize to."

"You say that every time."

"You arguing?"

He heard Tim give a satisfied groan as some muscle finally let go under the steamy hot water. "Not for a second."

Akbar stepped out and walked over to the line of sinks, smearing a hand back and forth to wipe the condensation from the sheet of stainless steel screwed to the wall. His hazy reflection still sported several smears of char.

"You so purdy, Akbar."

"Purdier than you, Two-Tall." He headed back into the shower to get the last of it.

"So not. You're jealous."

Akbar wasn't the least bit jealous. Yes, despite his lean height, Tim was handsome enough to sweep up any ladies he wanted.

But on his own, Akbar did pretty damn well himself. What he didn't have in height, he made up for with a proper smokejumper's muscled build. Mixed with his tan-dark Indian complexion, he did fine.

The real fun, of course, was when the two of them went cruising together. The women never knew what to make of the two of them side by side. The contrast kept them off balance enough to open even more doors.

He smiled as he toweled down. It also didn't hurt that their opening answer to "what do you do" was "I jump out of planes to fight forest fires."

Worked every damn time. God he loved this job.

# # #

The small town of Hood River, a winding half-an-hour down the mountain from the

MHA base camp, was hopping. Mid-June, colleges letting out. Students and the younger set of professors high-tailing it to the Gorge. They packed the bars and breweries and sidewalk cafes. Suddenly every other car on the street had a windsurfing board tied on the roof.

The snooty rich folks were up at the historic Timberline Lodge on Mount Hood itself, not far in the other direction from MHA. Down here it was a younger, thrill seeker set and you could feel the energy.

There were other restaurants in town that might have better pickings, but the Doghouse Inn was MHA tradition and it was a good luck charm—no smokie in his right mind messed with that. This was the bar where all of the MHA crew hung out. It didn't look like much from the outside, just a worn old brick building beaten by the Gorge's violent weather. Aged before its time, which had been long ago.

But inside was awesome. A long wooden bar stretched down one side with a half-jillion microbrew taps and a small but well-stocked kitchen at the far end. The dark wood paneling, even on the ceiling, was barely visible beneath thousands of pictures of doghouses sent from patrons all over the world. Miniature dachshunds in ornately decorated shoeboxes, massive Newfoundlands in backyard mansions that could easily house hundreds of their smaller kin, and everything in between. A gigantic Snoopy atop his doghouse in full Red Baron fighting gear dominated the far wall. Rumor said Shulz himself had been here two owners before and drawn it.

Tables were grouped close together, some for standing and drinking, others for sitting and eating.

"Amy, sweetheart!" Two-Tall called out as they entered the bar. The perky redhead came out from behind the bar to receive a hug from Tim. Akbar got one in turn, so he wasn't complaining. Cute as could be and about his height; her hugs were better than taking most women to bed. Of course, Gerald the cook and the bar's co-owner was big enough and strong enough to squish either Tim or Akbar if they got even a tiny step out of line with his wife. Gerald was one amazingly lucky man.

Akbar grabbed a Walking Man stout and

turned to assess the crowd. A couple of the air jocks were in. Carly and Steve were at a little table for two in the corner, obviously not interested in anyone's company but each others. Damn, that had happened fast. New guy on the base swept up one of the most beautiful women on the planet. One of these days he'd have to ask Steve how he'd done that. Or maybe not. It looked like they were settling in for the long haul; the big "M" was so not his own first choice.

Carly was also one of the best FBANs in the business. Akbar was a good Fire Behavior Analyst, had to be or he wouldn't have made it to first stick—lead smokie of the whole MHA crew. But Carly was something else again. He'd always found the Flame Witch, as she was often called, daunting and a bit scary besides; she knew the fire better than it did itself. Steve had latched on to one seriously driven lady. More power to him.

The selection of female tourists was especially good today, but no other smokies in yet. They'd be in soon enough…most of them had groaned awake and said they were coming as he and Two-Tall kicked their hallway doors, but not until they'd been on their way out—he and Tim had first pick. Actually some of the smokies were coming, others had told them quite succinctly where they could go—but hey, jumping into fiery hell is what they did for a living anyway, so no big change there.

A couple of the chopper pilots had nailed down a big table right in the middle of the bustling seating area: Jeannie, Mickey, and Vern. Good "field of fire" in the immediate area.

He and Tim headed over, but Akbar managed to snag the chair closest to the really hot lady with down-her-back curling dark-auburn hair at the next table over—set just right to see her profile easily. Hard shot, sitting there with her parents, but damn she was amazing. And if that was her mom, it said the woman would be good looking for a long time to come.

Two-Tall grimaced at him and Akbar offered him a comfortable "beat out your ass" grin. But this one didn't feel like that. Maybe it was the whole parental thing. He sat back and kept his mouth shut.

He made sure that Two-Tall could see his interest. That made Tim honor bound to try and cut Akbar out of the running.

# # #

Laura Jenson had spotted them coming into the restaurant. Her dad was only moments behind.

"Those two are walking like they just climbed off their first-ever horseback ride."

She had to laugh, they did. So stiff and awkward they barely managed to move upright. They didn't look like first-time wind-surfers, aching from the unexpected workout. They'd also walked in like they thought they were two gifts to god, which was even funnier. She turned away to avoid laughing in their faces. Guys who thought like that rarely appreciated getting a reality check.

A couple minutes later, at a nod from her dad, she did a careful sideways glance. Sure enough, they'd joined in with a group of friends who were seated at the next table behind her. The short one, shorter than she was by four or five inches, sat to one side. He was doing the old stare without staring routine, as if she were so naïve as to not recognize it. His ridiculously tall companion sat around the next turn of the table to her other side.

Then the tall one raised his voice enough to be heard easily over her dad's story about the latest goings-on at the local drone manufacturer. His company was the first one to be certified by the FAA for limited testing on wildfire and search-and-rescue overflights. She wanted to hear about it, but the tall guy had a deep voice that carried as if he were barrel-chested rather than pencil thin.

"Hell of fire, wasn't it? Where do you think we'll be jumping next?"

Smokies. Well, maybe they had some right to arrogance, but it didn't gain any ground with her.

"Please make it a small one," a woman who Laura couldn't see right behind her chimed in. "I wouldn't mind getting to sleep at least a couple times this summer if I'm gonna be flying you guys around."

Laura tried to listen to her dad, but the patter behind her was picking up speed.

Another guy, "Yeah, know what you

mean, Jeannie. I caught myself flying along trying to figure out how to fit crows and Stellar jays with little belly tanks to douse the flames. Maybe get a turkey vulture with a Type I heavy load classification."

"At least you weren't knocked down," Jeannie again. Laura liked her voice; she sounded fun. "Damn tree took out my rotor. They got it aloft, but maintenance hasn't signed it off for fire yet. They better have it done before the next call." A woman who knew no fear—or at least knew about getting back up on the horse.

A woman who flew choppers; that was kind of cool actually. Laura had thought about smokejumping, but not very hard. She enjoyed being down in the forest too much. She'd been born and bred to be a guide. And her job at Timberline Lodge let her do a lot of that.

Dad was working on the search-and-rescue testing. Said they could find a human body heat signature, even in deep trees.

"Hey," Laura finally managed to drag her attention wholly back to her parents. "If you guys need somewhere to test them, I'd love to play. As the Lodge's activities director, I'm down rivers, out on lakes, and leading mountain hikes on most days. All with tourists. And you know how much trouble they get into."

Mom laughed, she knew exactly what her daughter meant. Laura had come by the trade right down the matrilineal line. Grandma had been a fishing and hunting tour guide out of Nome, Alaska back when a woman had to go to Alaska to do more than be a teacher or nurse. Mom had done the same until she met a man from the lower forty-eight who promised they could ride horses almost year-round in Oregon. Laura had practically grown up on horseback, leading group rides deep into the Oregon Wilderness first with her mom and, by the time she was in her mid-teens, on her own.

They chatted about the newest drone technology for a while.

The guy with the big, deep voice finally faded away, one less guy to worry about hitting on her. But out of her peripheral vision, she could still see the other guy, the short one with the tan-dark skin, tight curly black hair, and shoulders like Atlas.

He'd teased the tall guy as they sat down and then gone silent. Not quite watching her; the same way she was not quite watching him.

Her dad missed what was going on, but her mom's smile was definitely giving her shit about it.

Available at fine retailers everywhere

More information at:
www.mlbuchman.com

Other works by M.L. Buchman

Angelo's Hearth

Where Dreams are Born
Where Dreams Reside
Maria's Christmas Table
Where Dreams Unfold
Where Dreams Are Written

Deities Anonymous

Cookbook from Hell: Reheated
Saviors 101

Thrillers

Swap Out!
One Chef!
Two Chef!

SF/F Titles

Nara
Monk's Maze

Printed in Great Britain
by Amazon